INSIGHT PUBLICA

Kozhikode, Kerala, India
www.insightpublica.com
e-mail: insightpublica@gmail.com
The Dark Lady of the Sonnets
Bernard Shaw
First Insight Publica Edition: December 2020

ISBN 978-93-90404-86-5

The Dark Lady of the Sonnets
Bernard Shaw

PREFACE TO
THE DARK LADY. OF
THE SONNETS

How the Play came to be Written

I had better explain why, in this little piece d'occasion, written for a performance in aid of the funds of the project for establishing a National Theatre as a memorial to Shakespear, I have identified the Dark Lady with Mistress Mary Fitton. First, let me say that I do not contend that the Dark Lady was Mary Fitton, because when the case in Mary's favor (or against her, if you please to consider that the Dark Lady was no better than she ought to have been) was complete, a portrait of Mary came to light and turned out to be that of a fair lady, not of a dark one. That settles the question, if the portrait is authentic, which I see no reason to doubt, and the lady's hair undyed, which is perhaps less certain. Shakespear rubbed in the lady's complexion in his sonnets mercilessly; for in his day black hair was as unpopular as red hair was in the early days of Queen Victoria. Any tinge lighter than raven black must be held fatal to the strongest claim to be the Dark Lady. And so, unless it can be shewn that Shakespear's sonnets exasperated Mary Fitton into dyeing her hair and getting painted in false colors, I must give up all pretence that my play is historical. The later suggestion of Mr Acheson that the Dark Lady, far from being a maid of honor, kept a tavern in Oxford and was the mother of Davenant the poet, is the one I should have adopted had I wished to be up to date. Why, then, did I introduce the Dark Lady as Mistress Fitton?

Well, I had two reasons. The play was not to have been written by me at all, but by Mrs Alfred Lyttelton; and it was she who suggested a scene of jealousy between Queen Elizabeth and the Dark Lady at the expense of the unfortunate Bard. Now this, if the Dark Lady was a maid of honor, was quite easy. If she were a tavern landlady, it would have strained all probability. So I stuck to Mary Fitton. But I had another and more personal reason. I was, in a manner, present at the birth of the Fitton theory. Its parent and I had become acquainted; and he used to consult me on obscure passages in the sonnets, on which, as far as I can remember, I never succeeded in throwing the faintest light, at a time when nobody else thought my opinion, on that or any other subject, of the slightest importance. I thought it would be friendly to immortalize him, as the silly literary saying is, much as Shakespear immortalized Mr W. H., as he said he would, simply by writing about him.

Let me tell the story formally.

Thomas Tyler

Throughout the eighties at least, and probably for some years before, the British Museum reading room was used daily by a gentleman of such astonishing and crushing ugliness that no one who had once seen him could ever thereafter forget him. He was of fair complexion, rather golden red than sandy; aged between forty-five and sixty; and dressed in frock coat and tall hat of presentable but never new appearance. His figure was rectangular, waistless, neckless, ankleless, of middle height, looking shortish because, though he was not particularly stout, there was nothing slender about him. His ugliness was not unamiable; it was accidental, external, excrescential. Attached to his face from the left ear to the point of his chin was a monstrous goitre, which hung down to his collar bone, and was very inadequately balanced by a smaller one on his right eyelid. Nature's malice was so overdone in his case that it somehow failed to produce the effect of repulsion it seemed to have aimed at. When you first met Thomas Tyler you could think of nothing else but whether surgery could really do nothing for him. But after a very brief acquaintance you never thought of his disfigurements at all, and talked to him as you might to Romeo or Lovelace; only, so many people, especially women, would not risk the preliminary ordeal, that he remained a man apart and a bachelor all his days. I am not to be frightened or prejudiced by a tumor; and I struck up a cordial acquaintance with him, in the course of which he kept me pretty closely on the track of his work at the Museum, in which I was then, like himself, a daily reader.

He was by profession a man of letters of an uncommercial kind. He was a specialist in pessimism; had made a translation of Ecclesiastes of which eight copies a year were sold; and followed up the pessimism of Shakespear and Swift with keen interest. He delighted in a hideous conception which he called the theory of the cycles, according to which the history of mankind and the universe keeps eternally repeating itself without the slightest variation throughout all eternity; so that he had lived and died and had his goitre before and would live and die and have it again and again and again. He liked to believe that nothing that happened to him was completely novel: he was persuaded that he often had some recollection of its previous occurrence in the last cycle. He hunted out allusions to this favorite theory in his three favorite pessimists. He tried his hand occasionally at deciphering ancient inscriptions, reading them as people seem to read the stars, by discovering bears and bulls and swords and goats where, as it seems to me, no sane human being can see anything but stars higgledy-piggledy. Next to the translation of Ecclesiastes, his magnum opus was his work on Shakespear's Sonnets, in which he accepted a previous identification of Mr W. H., the "onlie begetter" of the sonnets, with the Earl of Pembroke (William Herbert), and promulgated his own identification of Mistress Mary Fitton with the Dark Lady. Whether he was right or wrong about the Dark Lady did not matter urgently to me: she might have been Maria Tompkins for all I cared. But Tyler would have it that she was Mary Fitton; and he tracked Mary down from the first of her marriages in her teens to her tomb in Cheshire, whither he made a pilgrimage and whence returned in triumph with a picture of her statue, and the news that he was convinced she was a dark lady by traces of paint still discernible.

In due course he published his edition of the Sonnets, with the evidence he had collected. He lent me a copy of the book, which I never returned. But I reviewed it in the Pall Mall Gazette on the 7th of January 1886, and thereby let loose the Fitton theory in a wider circle of readers than the book could reach. Then Tyler died, sinking unnoted like a stone in the sea. I observed that Mr Acheson, Mrs Davenant's champion, calls him Reverend. It may very well be that he got his knowledge of Hebrew in reading for the Church; and there was always something of the clergyman or the schoolmaster in his dress and air. Possibly he may actually have been ordained. But he never told me that or anything else about his affairs; and his black pessimism would have shot him violently out of any church at present established in the West. We never talked about affairs: we talked about Shakespear, and the Dark Lady, and Swift, and Koheleth, and the cycles, and the mysterious moments when a feeling came over us that this had happened to us before, and about the forgeries of the Pentateuch which were offered for sale to the British Museum, and about literature and things of the spirit generally. He always came to my desk at the Museum and spoke to me about something or other, no doubt finding that people who were keen on this sort of conversation were rather scarce. He remains a vivid spot of memory in the void of my forgetfulness, a quite considerable and dignified soul in a grotesquely disfigured body.

Frank Harris

To the review in the Pall Mall Gazette I attribute, rightly or wrongly, the introduction of Mary Fitton to Mr Frank Harris. My reason for this is that Mr Harris wrote a play about Shakespear and Mary Fitton; and when I, as a pious duty to Tyler's ghost, reminded the world that it was to Tyler we owed the Fitton theory, Frank Harris, who clearly had not a notion of what had first put Mary into his head, believed, I think, that I had invented Tyler expressly for his discomfiture; for the stress I laid on Tyler's claims must have seemed unaccountable and perhaps malicious on the assumption that he was to me a mere name among the thousands of names in the British Museum catalogue. Therefore I make it clear that I had and have personal reasons for remembering Tyler, and for regarding myself as in some sort charged with the duty of reminding the world of his work. I am sorry for his sake that Mary's portrait is fair, and that Mr W. H. has veered round again from Pembroke to Southampton; but even so his work was not wasted: it is by exhausting all the hypotheses that we reach the verifiable one; and after all, the wrong road always leads somewhere.

Frank Harris's play was written long before mine. I read it in manuscript before the Shakespear Memorial National Theatre was mooted; and if there is anything except the Fitton theory (which is Tyler's property) in my play which is also in Mr Harris's it was I who annexed it from him and not he from me. It does not matter anyhow, because this play of mine is a brief trifle, and full of manifest impossibilities at that; whilst Mr Harris's play is serious both in size, intention, and quality. But there could not in the nature of things be much resemblance, because Frank conceives Shakespear to have been a broken-hearted, melancholy, enormously sentimental person, whereas I am convinced that he was very like myself: in fact, if I had been born in 1556 instead of in 1856, I should have taken to blank verse and given Shakespear a harder run for his money than all the other Elizabethans put together. Yet the success of Frank Harris's book on Shakespear gave me great delight.

To those who know the literary world of London there was a sharp stroke of ironic comedy in the irresistible verdict in its favor. In critical literature there is one prize that is always open to competition, one blue ribbon that always carries the highest critical rank with it. To win, you must write the best book of your generation on Shakespear. It is felt on all sides that to do this a certain fastidious refinement, a delicacy of taste, a correctness of manner and tone, and high academic distinction in addition to the indispensable scholarship and literary reputation, are needed; and men who pretend to these qualifications are constantly looked to with a gentle expectation that presently they will achieve the great feat. Now if there is a man on earth who is the utter contrary of everything that this description implies; whose very existence is an insult to the ideal it realizes; whose eye disparages, whose resonant voice denounces, whose cold shoulder jostles every decency, every delicacy, every amenity, every dignity, every sweet usage of that quiet life of mutual admiration in which perfect Shakespearian appreciation is expected to arise, that man is Frank Harris. Here is one who is extraordinarily qualified, by a range of sympathy and understanding that extends from the ribaldry of a buccaneer to the shyest tendernesses of the most sensitive poetry, to be all things to all men, yet whose proud humor it is to be to every man, provided the man is eminent and pretentious, the champion of his enemies. To the Archbishop he is an atheist, to the atheist a Catholic mystic, to the Bismarckian Imperialist an Anacharsis Klootz, to Anacharsis Klootz a Washington, to Mrs Proudie a Don Juan, to Aspasia a

John Knox: in short, to everyone his complement rather than his counterpart, his antagonist rather than his fellow-creature. Always provided, however, that the persons thus confronted are respectable persons. Sophie Perovskaia, who perished on the scaffold for blowing Alexander II to fragments, may perhaps have echoed Hamlet's

Oh God, Horatio, what a wounded name—
Things standing thus unknown—I leave behind!

but Frank Harris, in his Sonia, has rescued her from that injustice, and enshrined her among the saints. He has lifted the Chicago anarchists out of their infamy, and shewn that, compared with the Capitalism that killed them, they were heroes and martyrs. He has done this with the most unusual power of conviction. The story, as he tells it, inevitably and irresistibly displaces all the vulgar, mean, purblind, spiteful versions. There is a precise realism and an unsmiling, measured, determined sincerity which gives a strange dignity to the work of one whose fixed practice and ungovernable impulse it is to kick conventional dignity whenever he sees it.

Harris "durch Mitleid wissend"

Frank Harris is everything except a humorist, not, apparently, from stupidity, but because scorn overcomes humor in him. Nobody ever dreamt of reproaching Milton's Lucifer for not seeing the comic side of his fall; and nobody who has read Mr Harris's stories desires to have them lightened by chapters from the hand of Artemus Ward. Yet he knows the taste and the value of humor. He was one of the few men of letters who really appreciated Oscar Wilde, though he did not rally fiercely to Wilde's side until the world deserted Oscar in his ruin. I myself was present at a curious meeting between the two, when Harris, on the eve of the Queensberry trial, prophesied to Wilde with miraculous precision exactly what immediately afterwards happened to him, and warned him to leave the country. It was the first time within my knowledge that such a forecast proved true. Wilde, though under no illusion as to the folly of the quite unselfish suit-at-law he had been persuaded to begin, nevertheless so miscalculated the force of the social vengeance he was unloosing on himself that he fancied it could be stayed by putting up the editor of The Saturday Review (as Mr Harris then was) to declare that he considered Dorian Grey a highly moral book, which it certainly is. When Harris foretold him the truth, Wilde denounced him as a fainthearted friend who was failing him in his hour of need, and left the room in anger. Harris's idiosyncratic power of pity saved him from feeling or shewing the smallest resentment; and events presently proved to Wilde how insanely he had been advised in taking the action, and how accurately Harris had gauged the situation.

The same capacity for pity governs Harris's study of Shakespear, whom, as I have said, he pities too much; but that he is not insensible to humor is shewn not only by his appreciation of Wilde, but by the fact that the group of contributors who made his editorship of The Saturday Review so remarkable, and of whom I speak none the less highly because I happened to be one of them myself, were all, in their various ways, humorists.

"Sidney's Sister: Pembroke's Mother"

And now to return to Shakespear. Though Mr Harris followed Tyler in identifying Mary Fitton as the Dark Lady, and the Earl of Pembroke as the addressee of the other sonnets and the man who made love successfully to Shakespear's mistress, he very characteristically refuses to follow Tyler on one point, though for the life of me I cannot remember whether it was one of the surmises which Tyler published, or only one which he submitted to me to see what I would say about it, just as he used to submit difficult lines from the sonnets.

This surmise was that "Sidney's sister: Pembroke's mother" set Shakespear on to persuade Pembroke to marry, and that this was the explanation of those earlier sonnets which so persistently and unnaturally urged matrimony on Mr W. H. I take this to be one of the brightest of Tyler's ideas, because the persuasions in the sonnets are unaccountable and out of character unless they were offered to please somebody whom Shakespear desired to please, and who took a motherly interest in Pembroke. There is a further temptation in the theory for me. The most charming of all Shakespear's old women, indeed the most charming of all his women, young or old, is the Countess of Rousillon in All's Well That Ends Well. It has a certain individuality among them which suggests a portrait. Mr Harris will have it that all Shakespear's nice old women are drawn from his beloved mother; but I see no evidence whatever that Shakespear's mother was a particularly nice woman or that he was particularly fond of her. That she was a simple incarnation of extravagant maternal pride like the mother of Coriolanus in Plutarch, as Mr Harris asserts, I cannot believe: she is quite as likely to have borne her son a grudge for becoming "one of these harlotry players" and disgracing the Ardens. Anyhow, as a conjectural model for the Countess of Rousillon, I prefer that one of whom Jonson wrote

Sidney's sister: Pembroke's mother:
Death: ere thou has slain another,
Learnd and fair and good as she,
Time shall throw a dart at thee.

But Frank will not have her at any price, because his ideal Shakespear is rather like a sailor in a melodrama; and a sailor in a melodrama must adore his mother. I do not at all belittle such sailors. They are the emblems of human generosity; but Shakespear was not an emblem: he was a man and the author of Hamlet, who had no illusions about his mother. In weak moments one almost wishes he had.

Shakespear's Social Standing

On the vexed question of Shakespear's social standing Mr

Harris says that Shakespear "had not had the advantage of a middle-class training." I suggest that Shakespear missed this questionable advantage, not because he was socially too low to have attained to it, but because he conceived himself as belonging to the upper class from which our public school boys are now drawn. Let Mr Harris survey for a moment the field of contemporary journalism. He will see there some men who have the very characteristics from which he infers that Shakespear was at a social disadvantage through his lack of middle-class training. They are rowdy, ill-mannered, abusive, mischievous, fond of quoting obscene schoolboy anecdotes, adepts in that sort of blackmail which consists in mercilessly libelling and insulting every writer whose opinions are sufficiently heterodox to make it almost impossible for him to risk perhaps five years of a slender income by an appeal to a prejudiced orthodox jury; and they see nothing in all this cruel blackguardism but an uproariously jolly rag, although they are by no means without genuine literary ability, a love of letters, and even some artistic conscience. But he will find not one of the models of his type (I say nothing of mere imitators of it) below the rank that looks at the middle class, not humbly and enviously from below, but insolently from above. Mr Harris himself notes Shakespear's contempt for the tradesman and mechanic, and his incorrigible addiction to smutty jokes. He does us the public service of sweeping away the familiar plea of the Bardolatrous ignoramus, that Shakespear's coarseness was part of the manners of his time, putting his pen with precision on the one name, Spenser, that is necessary to expose such a libel on Elizabethan decency. There was nothing whatever to prevent Shakespear from being as decent as More was before him, or Bunyan after him, and as self-respecting as Raleigh or Sidney, except the tradition of his class, in which education or statesmanship may no doubt be acquired by those who have a turn for them, but in which insolence, derision, profligacy, obscene jesting, debt contracting, and rowdy mischievousness, give continual scandal to the pious, serious, industrious, solvent bourgeois. No other class is infatuated enough to believe that gentlemen are born and not made by a very elaborate process of culture. Even kings are taught and coached and drilled from their earliest boyhood to play their part. But the man of family (I am convinced that Shakespear took that view of himself) will plunge into society without a lesson in table manners, into politics without a lesson in history, into the city without a lesson in business, and into the army without a lesson in honor.

It has been said, with the object of proving Shakespear a laborer, that he could hardly write his name. Why? Because he "had not the advantage of a middle-class training." Shakespear himself tells us, through Hamlet, that gentlemen purposely wrote badly lest they should be mistaken for scriveners; but most of them, then as now, wrote badly because they could not write any better. In short, the whole range of Shakespear's foibles: the snobbishness, the naughtiness, the contempt for tradesmen and mechanics, the assumption that witty conversation can only mean smutty conversation, the flunkeyism towards social superiors and insolence towards social inferiors, the easy ways with servants which is seen not only between The Two Gentlemen of Verona and their valets, but in the affection and respect inspired by a great servant like Adam: all these are the characteristics of Eton and Harrow, not of the public elementary or private adventure school. They prove, as everything we know about Shakespear suggests, that he thought of the Shakespears and Ardens as families of consequence, and regarded himself as a gentleman under a cloud through his father's ill luck in business, and never for a moment as a man of the people. This is at once the explanation of and excuse for his snobbery. He was not a parvenu trying to cover his humble origin with a purchased coat of arms: he was a gentleman resuming what he conceived to be his natural position as soon as he gained the means to keep it up.

This Side Idolatry

There is another matter which I think Mr Harris should ponder. He says that Shakespear was but "little esteemed by his own generation." He even describes Jonson's description of his "little Latin and less Greek" as a sneer, whereas it occurs in an unmistakably sincere eulogy of Shakespear, written after his death, and is clearly meant to heighten the impression of Shakespear's prodigious natural endowments by pointing out that they were not due to scholastic acquirements. Now there is a sense in which it is true enough that Shakespear was too little esteemed by his own generation, or, for the matter of that, by any subsequent generation. The bargees on the Regent's Canal do not chant Shakespear's verses as the gondoliers in Venice are said to chant the verses of Tasso (a practice which was suspended for some reason during my stay in Venice: at least no gondolier ever did it in my hearing). Shakespear is no more a popular author than Rodin is a popular sculptor or Richard Strauss a popular composer. But Shakespear was certainly not such a fool as to expect the Toms, Dicks, and Harrys of his time to be any more interested in dramatic poetry than Newton, later on, expected them to be interested in fluxions. And when we come to the question whether Shakespear missed that assurance which all great men have had from the more capable and susceptible members of their generation that they were great men, Ben Jonson's evidence disposes of so improbable a notion at once and for ever. "I loved the man," says Ben, "this side idolatry, as well as any." Now why in the name of common sense should he have made that qualification unless there had been, not only idolatry, but idolatry fulsome enough to irritate Jonson into an express disavowal of it? Jonson, the bricklayer, must have felt sore sometimes when Shakespear spoke and wrote of bricklayers as his inferiors. He must have felt it a little hard that being a better scholar, and perhaps a braver and tougher man physically than Shakespear, he was not so successful or so well liked. But in spite of this he praised Shakespear to the utmost stretch of his powers of eulogy: in fact, notwithstanding his disclaimer, he did not stop "this side idolatry." If, therefore, even Jonson felt himself forced to clear himself of extravagance and absurdity in his appreciation of Shakespear, there must have been many people about who idolized Shakespear as American ladies idolize Paderewski, and who carried Bardolatry, even in the Bard's own time, to an extent that threatened to make his reasonable admirers ridiculous.

Shakespear's Pessimism

I submit to Mr Harris that by ruling out this idolatry, and its possible effect in making Shakespear think that his public would stand anything from him, he has ruled out a far more plausible explanation of the faults of such a play as Timon of Athens than his theory that Shakespear's passion for the Dark Lady "cankered and took on proud flesh in him, and tortured him to nervous breakdown and madness." In Timon the intellectual bankruptcy is obvious enough: Shakespear tried once too often to make a play out of the cheap pessimism which is thrown into despair by a comparison of actual human nature with theoretical morality, actual law and administration with abstract justice, and so forth. But Shakespear's perception of the fact that all men, judged by the moral standard which they apply to others and by which they justify their punishment of others, are fools and scoundrels, does not date from the Dark Lady complication: he seems to have been born with it. If in The Comedy of Errors and A Midsummer Night's Dream the persons of the drama are not quite so ready for treachery and murder as Laertes and even Hamlet himself (not to mention the procession of ruffians who pass through the latest plays) it is certainly not because they have any more re-gard for law or religion. There is only one place in Shakespear's plays where the sense of shame is used as a human attribute; and that is where Hamlet is ashamed, not of anything he himself has done, but of his mother's relations with his uncle. This scene is an unnatural one: the son's reproaches to his mother, even the fact of his being able to discuss the subject with her, is more repulsive than her relations with her deceased husband's brother.

Here, too, Shakespear betrays for once his religious sense by making Hamlet, in his agony of shame, declare that his mother's conduct makes "sweet religion a rhapsody of words." But for that passage we might almost suppose that the feeling of Sunday morning in the country which Orlando describes so perfectly in As You Like It was the beginning and end of Shakespear's notion of religion. I say almost, because Isabella in Measure for Measure has religious charm, in spite of the conventional theatrical assumption that female religion means an inhumanly ferocious chastity. But for the most part Shakespear differentiates his heroes from his villains much more by what they do than by what they are. Don John in Much Ado is a true villain: a man with a malicious will; but he is too dull a duffer to be of any use in a leading part; and when we come to the great villains like Macbeth, we find, as Mr Harris points out, that they are precisely identical with the heroes: Macbeth is only Hamlet incongruously committing murders and engaging in hand-to-hand combats. And Hamlet, who does not dream of apologizing for the three murders he commits, is always apologizing because he has not yet committed a fourth, and finds, to his great bewilderment, that he does not want to commit it. "It cannot be," he says, "but I am pigeon-livered, and lack gall to make oppression bitter; else, ere this, I should have fatted all the region kites with this slave's offal." Really one is tempted to suspect that when Shylock asks "Hates any man the thing he would not kill?" he is expressing the natural and proper sentiments of the human race as Shakespear understood them, and not the vindictiveness of a stage Jew.

Gaiety of Genius

In view of these facts, it is dangerous to cite Shakespear's pessimism as evidence of the despair of a heart broken by the Dark Lady. There is an irrepressible gaiety of genius which enables it to bear the whole weight of the world's misery without blenching. There is a laugh always ready to avenge its tears of discouragement. In the lines which Mr Harris quotes only to declare that he can make nothing of them, and to condemn them as out of character, Richard III, immediately after pitying himself because

> There is no creature loves me
> And if I die no soul will pity me,
> adds, with a grin,

> Nay, wherefore should they, since that I myself
> Find in myself no pity for myself?

Let me again remind Mr Harris of Oscar Wilde. We all dreaded to read De Profundis: our instinct was to stop our ears, or run away from the wail of a broken, though by no means contrite, heart. But we were throwing away our pity. De Profundis was de profundis indeed: Wilde was too good a dramatist to throw away so powerful an effect; but none the less it was de profundis in excelsis. There was more laughter between the lines of that book than in a thousand farces by men of no genius. Wilde, like Richard and Shakespear, found in himself no pity for himself. There is nothing that marks the born dramatist more unmistakably than this discovery of comedy in his own misfortunes almost in proportion to the pathos with which the ordinary man announces their tragedy. I cannot for the life of me see the broken heart in Shakespear's latest works. "Hark, hark! the lark at heaven's gate sings" is not the lyric of a broken man; nor is Cloten's comment that if Imogen does not appreciate it, "it is a vice in her ears which horse hairs, and cats' guts, and the voice of unpaved eunuch to boot, can never amend," the sally of a saddened one. Is it not clear that to the last there was in Shakespear an incorrigible divine levity, an inexhaustible joy that derided sorrow? Think of the poor Dark Lady having to stand up to this unbearable power of extracting a grim fun from everything. Mr Harris writes as if Shakespear did all the suffering and the Dark Lady all the cruelty. But why does he not put himself in the Dark Lady's place for a moment as he has put himself so successfully in Shakespear's? Imagine her reading the hundred and thirtieth sonnet!

> My mistress' eyes are nothing like the sun;
> Coral is far more red than her lips' red;
> If snow be white, why then her breasts are dun;
> If hairs be wire, black wires grow on her head;
> I have seen roses damasked, red and white,
> But no such roses see I in her cheeks;
> And in some perfumes is there more delight
> Than in the breath that from my mistress reeks.
> I love to hear her speak; yet well I know
> That music hath a far more pleasing sound.
> I grant I never saw a goddess go:
> My mistress, when she walks, treads on the ground.
> And yet, by heaven, I think my love as rare
> As any she belied with false compare.

Take this as a sample of the sort of compliment from which she was never for a moment safe with SHAKESPEAR. Bear in mind that she was not a comedian; that the Elizabethan fashion of treating brunettes as ugly woman must have made her rather sore on the subject of her complexion; that no human being, male or female, can conceivably enjoy being chaffed on that point in the fourth couplet about the perfumes; that Shakespear's revulsions, as the sonnet immediately preceding shews, were as violent as his ardors, and were expressed with the realistic power and horror that makes Hamlet say that the heavens got sick when they saw the queen's conduct; and then ask Mr Harris whether any woman could have stood it for long, or have thought the "sugred" compliment worth the cruel wounds, the cleaving of the heart in twain, that seemed to Shakespear as natural and amusing a reaction as the burlesquing of his heroics by Pistol, his sermons by Falstaff, and his poems by Cloten and Touchstone.

Jupiter and Semele

This does not mean that Shakespear was cruel: evidently he was not; but it was not cruelty that made Jupiter reduce Semele to ashes: it was the fact that he could not help being a god nor she help being a mortal. The one thing Shakespear's passion for the Dark Lady was not, was what Mr Harris in one passage calls it: idolatrous. If it had been, she might have been able to stand it. The man who "dotes yet doubts, suspects, yet strongly loves," is tolerable even by a spoilt and tyrannical mistress; but what woman could possibly endure a man who dotes without doubting; who knows, and who is hugely amused at the absurdity of his infatuation for a woman of whose mortal imperfections not one escapes him: a man always exchanging grins with Yorick's skull, and inviting "my lady" to laugh at the sepulchral humor of the fact that though she paint an inch thick (which the Dark Lady may have done), to Yorick's favor she must come at last. To the Dark Lady he must sometimes have seemed cruel beyond description: an intellectual Caliban. True, a Caliban who could say

> Be not afeard: the isle is full of noises
> Sounds and sweet airs that give delight and hurt not.
> Sometimes a thousand twangling instruments
> Will hum about mine ears; and sometimes voices,
> That, if I then had waked after long sleep
> Will make me sleep again; and then, in dreaming,
> The clouds, methought, would open and shew riches
> Ready to drop on me: that when I wak'd
> I cried to dream again.

which is very lovely; but the Dark Lady may have had that

vice in her ears which Cloten dreaded: she may not have seen
the beauty of it, whereas there can be no doubt at all that of "My
mistress' eyes are nothing like the sun," &c., not a word was lost
on her.

And is it to be supposed that Shakespear was too stupid or
too modest not to see at last that it was a case of Jupiter and Semele? Shakespear was most certainly not modest in that sense.
The timid cough of the minor poet was never heard from him.

Not marble, nor the gilded monuments

Of princes, shall outlive this powerful rhyme

is only one out of a dozen passages in which he (possibly with
a keen sense of the fun of scandalizing the modest coughers)
proclaimed his place and his power in "the wide world dream-
ing of things to come." The Dark Lady most likely thought this
side of him insufferably conceited; for there is no reason to suppose that she liked his plays any better than Minna Wagner liked
Richard's music dramas: as likely as not, she thought The Spanish Tragedy worth six Hamlets. He was not stupid either: if his
class limitations and a profession that cut him off from actual
participation in great affairs of State had not confined his op-
portunities of intellectual and political training to private conversation and to the Mermaid Tavern, he would probably have
become one of the ablest men of his time instead of being merely
its ablest playwright. One might surmise that Shakespear found
out that the Dark Lady's brains could no more keep pace with
his than Anne Hathaway's, if there were any evidence that their
friendship ceased when he stopped writing sonnets to her. As
a matter of fact the consolidation of a passion into an enduring
intimacy generally puts an end to sonnets.

That the Dark Lady broke Shakespear's heart, as Mr Harris
will have it she did, is an extremely unShakespearian hypothesis.
"Men have died from time to time, and worms have eaten them;
but not for love," says Rosalind. Richard of Gloster, into whom

Shakespear put all his own impish superiority to vulgar sentiment, exclaims

> And this word "love," which greybeards call divine,
> Be resident in men like one another
> And not in me: I am myself alone.

Hamlet has not a tear for Ophelia: her death moves him to fierce disgust for the sentimentality of Laertes by her grave; and when he discusses the scene with Horatio immediately after, he utterly forgets her, though he is sorry he forgot himself, and jumps at the proposal of a fencing match to finish the day with. As against this view Mr Harris pleads Romeo, Orsino, and even Antonio; and he does it so penetratingly that he convinces you that Shakespear did betray himself again and again in these characters; but self-betrayal is one thing; and self-portrayal, as in Hamlet and Mercutio, is another. Shakespear never "saw himself," as actors say, in Romeo or Orsino or Antonio. In Mr Harris's own play Shakespear is presented with the most pathetic tenderness. He is tragic, bitter, pitiable, wretched and broken among a robust crowd of Jonsons and Elizabeths; but to me he is not Shakespear because I miss the Shakespearian irony and the Shakespearian gaiety. Take these away and Shakespear is no longer Shakespear: all the bite, the impetus, the strength, the grim delight in his own power of looking terrible facts in the face with a chuckle, is gone; and you have nothing left but that most depressing of all things: a victim. Now who can think of Shakespear as a man with a grievance? Even in that most thoroughgoing and inspired of all Shakespear's loves: his love of music (which Mr Harris has been the first to appreciate at anything like its value), there is a dash of mockery. "Spit in the hole, man; and tune again." "Divine air! Now is his soul ravished. Is it not strange that sheep's guts should hale the souls out of men's bodies?" "An he had been a dog that should have howled thus, they would have hanged him." There is just as much Shakespear here as in the inevitable quotation about the sweet south and the bank of violets.

I lay stress on this irony of Shakespear's, this impish rejoicing in pessimism, this exultation in what breaks the hearts of common men, not only because it is diagnostic of that immense energy of life which we call genius, but because its omission is the one glaring defect in Mr Harris's otherwise extraordinarily penetrating book. Fortunately, it is an omission that does not disable the book as (in my judgment) it disabled the hero of the play, because Mr Harris left himself out of his play, whereas he pervades his book, mordant, deep-voiced, and with an unconquerable style which is the man.

The Idol of the Bardolaters

There is even an advantage in having a book on Shakespear with the Shakespearian irony left out of account. I do not say that the missing chapter should not be added in the next edition: the hiatus is too great: it leaves the reader too uneasy before this touching picture of a writhing worm substituted for the invulnerable giant. But it is none the less probable that in no other way could Mr Harris have got at his man as he has. For, after all, what is the secret of the hopeless failure of the academic Bardolaters to give us a credible or even interesting Shakespear, and the easy triumph of Mr Harris in giving us both? Simply that Mr Harris has assumed that he was dealing with a man, whilst the others have assumed that they were writing about a god, and have therefore rejected every consideration of fact, tradition, or interpretation, that pointed to any human imperfection in their hero. They thus leave themselves with so little material that they are forced to begin by saying that we know very little about SHAKESPEAR.   As a matter of fact, with the plays and sonnets in our hands, we know much more about Shakespear than we know about Dickens or Thackeray: the only difficulty is that we deliberately suppress it because it proves that Shakespear was not only very unlike the conception of a god current in Clapham, but was not, according to the same reckoning, even a respectable man. The academic view starts with a Shakespear who was not scurrilous; therefore the verses about "lousy Lucy" cannot have been written by him, and the cognate passages in the plays are either strokes of character-drawing or gags interpolated by the actors. This ideal Shakespear was too well behaved to get drunk; therefore the tradition that his death was hastened by a drinking bout with Jonson and Drayton must be rejected, and the remorse of Cassio treated as a thing observed, not experienced: nay, the disgust of Hamlet at the drinking customs of Denmark is taken to establish Shakespear as the superior of Alexander in self-control, and the greatest of teetotallers.

Now this system of inventing your great man to start with, and then rejecting all the materials that do not fit him, with the ridiculous result that you have to declare that there are no materials at all (with your waste-paper basket full of them), ends in leaving Shakespear with a much worse character than he deserves. For though it does not greatly matter whether he wrote the lousy Lucy lines or not, and does not really matter at all whether he got drunk when he made a night of it with Jonson and Drayton, the sonnets raise an unpleasant question which does matter a good deal; and the refusal of the academic Bardolaters to discuss or even mention this question has had the effect of producing a silent verdict against Shakespear. Mr Harris tackles the question openly, and has no difficulty whatever in convincing us that Shakespear was a man of normal constitution sexually, and was not the victim of that most cruel and pitiable of all the freaks of nature: the freak which transposes the normal aim of the affections. Silence on this point means condemnation; and the condemnation has been general throughout the present generation, though it only needed Mr Harris's fearless handling of the matter to sweep away what is nothing but a morbid and very disagreeable modern fashion. There is always some stock accusation brought against eminent persons. When I was a boy every well-known man was accused of beating his wife. Later on, for some unexplained reason, he was accused of psychopathic derangement. And this fashion is retrospective. The cases of Shakespear and Michel Angelo are cited as proving that every genius of the first magnitude was a sufferer; and both here and in Germany there are circles in which such derangement is grotesquely reverenced as part of the stigmata of heroic powers. All of which is gross nonsense. Unfortunately, in Shakespear's case, prudery, which cannot prevent the accusation from being whispered, does prevent the refutation from being shouted. Mr Harris, the deep-voiced, refuses to be silenced. He dismisses with proper contempt the stupidity which places an outrageous construction on Shakespear's apologies in the sonnets for neglecting that "perfect ceremony" of love which consists in returning calls and making protestations and giving presents and paying the trumpery attentions which men of genius always refuse to bother about, and to which touchy people who have no genius attach so much importance. No leader who had not been tampered with by the psychopathic monomaniacs could ever put any construction but the obvious and innocent one on these passages. But the general vocabulary of the sonnets to Pembroke (or whoever "Mr W. H." really was) is so overcharged according to modern ideas that a reply on the general case is necessary.

Shakespear's alleged
Sycophancy and Perversion

That reply, which Mr Harris does not hesitate to give, is twofold: first, that Shakespear was, in his attitude towards earls, a sycophant; and, second, that the normality of Shakespear's sexual constitution is only too well attested by the excessive susceptibility to the normal impulse shewn in the whole mass of his writings. This latter is the really conclusive reply. In the case of Michel Angelo, for instance, one must admit that if his works are set beside those of Titian or Paul Veronese, it is impossible not to be struck by the absence in the Florentine of that susceptibility to feminine charm which pervades the pictures of the Venetians. But, as Mr Harris points out (though he does not use this particular illustration) Paul Veronese is an anchorite compared to Shakespear. The language of the sonnets addressed to Pembroke, extravagant as it now seems, is the language of compliment and fashion, transfigured no doubt by Shakespear's verbal magic, and hyperbolical, as Shakespear always seems to people who cannot conceive so vividly as he, but still unmistakable for anything else than the expression of a friendship delicate enough to be wounded, and a manly loyalty deep enough to be outraged. But the language of the sonnets to the Dark Lady is the language of passion: their cruelty shews it. There is no evidence that Shakespear was capable of being unkind in cold blood. But in his revulsions from love, he was bitter, wounding, even ferocious; sparing neither himself nor the unfortunate woman whose only offence was that she had reduced the great man to the common human denominator.

In seizing on these two points Mr Harris has made so sure a stroke, and placed his evidence so featly that there is nothing left for me to do but to plead that the second is sounder than the first, which is, I think, marked by the prevalent mistake as to Shakespear's social position, or, if you prefer it, the confusion between his actual social position as a penniless tradesman's son taking to the theatre for a livelihood, and his own conception of himself as a gentleman of good family. I am prepared to contend that though Shakespear was undoubtedly sentimental in his expressions of devotion to Mr W. H. even to a point which nowadays makes both ridiculous, he was not sycophantic if Mr W. H. was really attractive and promising, and Shakespear deeply attached to him. A sycophant does not tell his patron that his fame will survive, not in the renown of his own actions, but in the sonnets of his sycophant. A sycophant, when his patron cuts him out in a love affair, does not tell his patron exactly what he thinks of him. Above all, a sycophant does not write to his patron precisely as he feels on all occasions; and this rare kind of sincerity is all over the sonnets. Shakespear, we are told, was "a very civil gentleman." This must mean that his desire to please people and be liked by them, and his reluctance to hurt their feelings, led him into amiable flattery even when his feelings were not strongly stirred. If this be taken into account along with the fact that Shakespear conceived and expressed all his emotions with a vehemence that sometimes carried him into ludicrous extravagance, making Richard offer his kingdom for a horse and Othello declare of Cassio that

> Had all his hairs been lives, my great revenge
> Had stomach for them all,

we shall see more civility and hyperbole than sycophancy even in the earlier and more coldblooded sonnets.

Shakespear and Democracy

Now take the general case pled against Shakespear as an enemy of democracy by Tolstoy, the late Ernest Crosbie and others, and endorsed by Mr Harris. Will it really stand fire? Mr Harris emphasizes the passages in which Shakespear spoke of mechanics and even of small master tradesmen as base persons whose clothes were greasy, whose breath was rank, and whose political imbecility and caprice moved Coriolanus to say to the Roman Radical who demanded at least "good words" from him

> He that will give good words to thee will flatter
> Beneath abhorring.

But let us be honest. As political sentiments these lines are an abomination to every democrat. But suppose they are not political sentiments! Suppose they are merely a record of observed fact. John Stuart Mill told our British workmen that they were mostly liars. Carlyle told us all that we are mostly fools. Matthew Arnold and Ruskin were more circumstantial and more abusive. Everybody, including the workers themselves, know that they are dirty, drunken, foul-mouthed, ignorant, gluttonous, prejudiced: in short, heirs to the peculiar ills of poverty and slavery, as well as co-heirs with the plutocracy to all the failings of human nature. Even Shelley admitted, 200 years after Shakespear wrote Coriolanus, that universal suffrage was out of the question. Surely the real test, not of Democracy, which was not a live political issue in Shakespear's time, but of impartiality in judging classes, which is what one demands from a great human poet, is not that he should flatter the poor and denounce the rich, but that he should weigh them both in the same balance. Now whoever will read Lear and Measure for Measure will find stamped on his mind such an appalled sense of the danger of dressing man in a little brief authority, such a merciless stripping of the purple from the "poor, bare, forked animal" that calls itself a king and fancies itself a god, that one wonders what was the real nature of the mysterious restraint that kept "Eliza and our James" from teaching Shakespear to be civil to crowned heads, just as one wonders why Tolstoy was allowed to go free when so many less terrible levellers went to the galleys or Siberia. From the mature Shakespear we get no such scenes of village snobbery as that between the stage country gentleman Alexander Iden and the stage Radical Jack Cade. We get the shepherd in As You Like It, and many honest, brave, human, and loyal servants, beside the inevitable comic ones. Even in the Jingo play, Henry V, we get Bates and Williams drawn with all respect and honor as normal rank and file men. In Julius Caesar, Shakespear went to work with a will when he took his cue from Plutarch in glorifying regicide and transfiguring the republicans. Indeed hero-worshippers have never forgiven him for belittling Caesar and failing to see that side of his assassination which made Goethe denounce it as the most senseless of crimes. Put the play beside the Charles I of Wills, in which Cromwell is written down to a point at which the Jack Cade of Henry VI becomes a hero in comparison; and then believe, if you can, that Shakespear was one of them that "crook the pregnant hinges of the knee where thrift may follow fawning." Think of Rosencrantz, Guildenstern, Osric, the fop who annoyed Hotspur, and a dozen passages concerning such people! If such evidence can prove anything (and Mr Harris relies throughout on such evidence) Shakespear loathed courtiers.

If, on the other hand, Shakespear's characters are mostly members of the leisured classes, the same thing is true of Mr Harris's own plays and mine. Industrial slavery is not compatible with that freedom of adventure, that personal refinement and intellectual culture, that scope of action, which the higher and subtler drama demands.

Even Cervantes had finally to drop Don Quixote's troubles with innkeepers demanding to be paid for his food and lodging, and make him as free of economic difficulties as Amadis de Gaul. Hamlet's experiences simply could not have happened to a plumber. A poor man is useful on the stage only as a blind man is: to excite sympathy. The poverty of the apothecary in Romeo and Juliet produces a great effect, and even points the sound moral that a poor man cannot afford to have a conscience; but if all the characters of the play had been as poor as he, it would have been nothing but a melodrama of the sort that the Sicilian players gave us here; and that was not the best that lay in Shakespear's power. When poverty is abolished, and leisure and grace of life become general, the only plays surviving from our epoch which will have any relation to life as it will be lived then will be those in which none of the persons represented are troubled with want of money or wretched drudgery. Our plays of poverty and squalor, now the only ones that are true to the life of the majority of living men, will then be classed with the records of misers and monsters, and read only by historical students of social pathology.

Then consider Shakespear's kings and lords and gentlemen! Would even John Ball or Jeremiah complain that they are flattered? Surely a more mercilessly exposed string of scoundrels never crossed the stage. The very monarch who paralyzes a rebel by appealing to the divinity that hedges a king, is a drunken and sensual assassin, and is presently killed contemptuously before our eyes in spite of his hedge of divinity. I could write as convincing a chapter on Shakespear's Dickensian prejudice against the throne and the nobility and gentry in general as Mr Harris or Ernest Crosbie on the other side. I could even go so far as to contend that one of Shakespear's defects is his lack of an intelligent comprehension of feudalism. He had of course no prevision of democratic Collectivism. He was, except in the commonplaces of war and patriotism, a privateer through and through. Nobody in his plays, whether king or citizen, has any civil public business or conception of such a thing, except in the method of appointing constables, to the abuses in which he called attention quite in the vein of the Fabian Society. He was concerned about drunkenness and about the idolatry and hypocrisy of our judicial system; but his implied remedy was personal sobriety and freedom from idolatrous illusion in so far as he had any remedy at all, and did not merely despair of human nature. His first and last word on parliament was "Get thee glass eyes, and, like a scurvy politician, seem to see the thing thou dost not." He had no notion of the feeling with which the land nationalizers of today regard the fact that he was a party to the enclosure of common lands at Wellcome. The explanation is, not a general deficiency in his mind, but the simple fact that in his day what English land needed was individual appropriation and cultivation, and what the English Constitution needed was the incorporation of Whig principles of individual liberty.

Shakespear and the British Public

I have rejected Mr Harris's view that Shakespear died broken-hearted of "the pangs of love despised." I have given my reasons for believing that Shakespear died game, and indeed in a state of levity which would have been considered unbecoming in a bishop. But Mr Harris's evidence does prove that Shakespear had a grievance and a very serious one. He might have been jilted by ten dark ladies and been none the worse for it; but his treatment by the British Public was another matter. The idolatry which exasperated Ben Jonson was by no means a popular movement; and, like all such idolatries, it was excited by the magic of Shakespear's art rather than by his views.

He was launched on his career as a successful playwright by the Henry VI trilogy, a work of no originality, depth, or subtlety except the originality, depth, and subtlety of the feelings and fancies of the common people. But Shakespear was not satisfied with this. What is the use of being Shakespear if you are not allowed to express any notions but those of Autolycus? Shakespear did not see the world as Autolycus did: he saw it, if not exactly as Ibsen did (for it was not quite the same world), at least with much of Ibsen's power of penetrating its illusions and idolatries, and with all Swift's horror of its cruelty and uncleanliness.

Now it happens to some men with these powers that they are forced to impose their fullest exercise on the world because they cannot produce popular work. Take Wagner and Ibsen for instance! Their earlier works are no doubt much cheaper than their later ones; still, they were not popular when they were written. The alternative of doing popular work was never really open to them: had they stooped they would have picked up less than they snatched from above the people's heads. But Handel and Shakespear were not held to their best in this way. They could turn out anything they were asked for, and even heap up the measure. They reviled the British Public, and never forgave it for ignoring their best work and admiring their splendid commonplaces; but they produced the commonplaces all the same, and made them sound magnificent by mere brute faculty for their art. When Shakespear was forced to write popular plays to save his theatre from ruin, he did it mutinously, calling the plays "As

You Like It," and "Much Ado About Nothing." All the same, he did it so well that to this day these two genial vulgarities are the main Shakespearian stock-in-trade of our theatres. Later on Burbage's power and popularity as an actor enabled Shakespear to free himself from the tyranny of the box office, and to express himself more freely in plays consisting largely of monologue to be spoken by a great actor from whom the public would stand a good deal. The history of Shakespear's tragedies has thus been the history of a long line of famous actors, from Burbage and Betterton to Forbes Robertson; and the man of whom we are told that "when he would have said that Richard died, and cried A horse! A horse! he Burbage cried" was the father of nine generations of Shakespearian playgoers, all speaking of Garrick's Richard, and Kean's Othello, and Irving's Shylock, and Forbes Robertson's Hamlet without knowing or caring how much these had to do with Shakespear's Richard and Othello and so forth. And the plays which were written without great and predominant parts, such as Troilus and Cressida, All's Well That Ends Well, and Measure for Measure, have dropped on our stage as dead as the second part of Goethe's Faust or Ibsen's Emperor or Galilean.

Here, then, Shakespear had a real grievance; and though it is a sentimental exaggeration to describe him as a broken-hearted man in the face of the passages of reckless jollity and serenely happy poetry in his latest plays, yet the discovery that his most serious work could reach success only when carried on the back of a very fascinating actor who was enormously overcharging his part, and that the serious plays which did not contain parts big enough to hold the overcharge were left on the shelf, amply accounts for the evident fact that Shakespear did not end his life in a glow of enthusiastic satisfaction with mankind and with the theatre, which is all that Mr Harris can allege in support of his broken-heart theory. But even if Shakespear had had no failures, it was not possible for a man of his powers to observe the political and moral conduct of his contemporaries without perceiving that they were incapable of dealing with the problems raised by their own civilization, and that their attempts to carry out the codes of law and to practise the religions offered to them by great prophets and law-givers were and still are so foolish that we now call for The Superman, virtually a new species, to rescue the world from mismanagement. This is the real sorrow of great men; and in the face of it the notion that when a great man speaks bitterly or looks melancholy he must be troubled by a disappointment in love seems to me sentimental trifling.

If I have carried the reader with me thus far, he will find that trivial as this little play of mine is, its sketch of Shakespear is more complete than its levity suggests. Alas! its appeal for a National Theatre as a monument to Shakespear failed to touch the very stupid people who cannot see that a National Theatre is worth having for the sake of the National Soul. I had unfortunately represented Shakespear as treasuring and using (as I do myself) the jewels of unconsciously musical speech which common people utter and throw away every day; and this was taken as a disparagement of Shakespear's "originality." Why was I born with such contemporaries? Why is Shakespear made ridiculous by such a posterity?

The Dark Lady of The Sonnets was first performed at the Haymarket Theatre, on the afternoon of Thursday, the 24th November 1910, by Mona Limerick as the Dark Lady, Suzanne Sheldon as Queen Elizabeth, Granville Barker as Shakespear, and Hugh Tabberer as the Warder.

THE DARK LADY. OF THE SONNETS

Fin de siecle 15-1600. Midsummer night on the terrace of the Palace at Whitehall, overlooking the Thames. The Palace clock chimes four quarters and strikes eleven.

A Beefeater on guard. A Cloaked Man approaches.

THE BEEFEATER.	Stand. Who goes there? Give the word.
THE MAN.	Marry! I cannot. I have clean forgotten it.
THE BEEFEATER.	Then cannot you pass here. What is your business? Who are you? Are you a true man?
THE MAN.	Far from it, Master Warder. I am not the same man two days together: sometimes Adam, sometimes Benvolio, and anon the Ghost.
THE BEEFEATER.	[recoiling] A ghost! Angels and ministers of grace defend us!

THE MAN. Well said, Master Warder. With your leave I will set that down in writing; for I have a very poor and unhappy brain for remembrance. [He takes out his tablets and writes]. Methinks this is a good scene, with you on your lonely watch, and I approaching like a ghost in the moonlight. Stare not so amazedly at me; but mark what I say. I keep tryst here to-night with a dark lady. She promised to bribe the warder. I gave her the wherewithal: four tickets for the Globe Theatre.

THE BEEFEATER. Plague on her! She gave me two only.

THE MAN. [detaching a tablet] My friend: present this tablet, and you will be welcomed at any time when the plays of Will Shakespear are in hand. Bring your wife. Bring your friends. Bring the whole garrison. There is ever plenty of room.

THE BEEFEATER. I care not for these new-fangled plays. No man can understand a word of them. They are all talk. Will you not give me a pass for The Spanish Tragedy?

THE MAN. To see The Spanish Tragedy one pays, my friend. Here are the means. [He gives him a piece of gold].

THE BEEFEATER. [overwhelmed] Gold! Oh, sir, you are a better paymaster than your dark lady.

THE MAN. Women are thrifty, my friend.

THE BEEFEATER. Tis so, sir. And you have to consider that the most open handed of us must een cheapen that which we buy every day. This lady has to make a present to a warder nigh every night of her life.

THE MAN. [turning pale] I'll not believe it.

THE BEEFEATER. Now you, sir, I dare be sworn, do not have an adventure like this twice in the year.

THE MAN. Villain: wouldst tell me that my dark lady hath ever done thus before? that she maketh occasions to meet other men?

THE BEEFEATER. Now the Lord bless your innocence, sir, do you think you are the only pretty man in the world? A merry lady, sir: a warm bit of stuff. Go to: I'll not see her pass a deceit on a gentleman that hath given me the first piece of gold I ever handled.

THE MAN. Master Warder: is it not a strange thing that we, knowing that all women are false, should be amazed to find our own particular drab no better than the rest?

THE BEEFEATER. Not all, sir. Decent bodies, many of them.

THE MAN. [intolerantly] No. All false. All. If thou

deny it, thou liest.

THE BEEFEATER. You judge too much by the Court, sir. There, indeed, you may say of frailty that its name is woman.

THE MAN. [pulling out his tablets again] Prithee say that again: that about frailty: the strain of music.

THE BEEFEATER. What strain of music, sir? I'm no musician, God knows.

THE MAN. There is music in your soul: many of your degree have it very notably. [Writing] "Frailty: thy name is woman!" [Repeating it affectionately] "Thy name is woman."

THE BEEFEATER. Well, sir, it is but four words. Are you a snapper-up of such unconsidered trifles?

THE MAN. [eagerly] Snapper-up of—[he gasps] Oh! Immortal phrase! [He writes it down]. This man is a greater than I.

THE BEEFEATER. You have my lord Pembroke's trick, sir.

THE MAN. Like enough: he is my near friend. But what call you his trick?

THE BEEFEATER. Making sonnets by moonlight. And to the same lady too.

THE MAN. No!

THE BEEFEATER. Last night he stood here on your errand, and in your shoes.

THE MAN. Thou, too, Brutus! And I called him

friend!

THE BEEFEATER.   Tis ever so, sir.

THE MAN.   Tis ever so. Twas ever so. [He turns away, overcome]. Two Gentlemen of Verona! Judas! Judas!!

THE BEEFEATER.   Is he so bad as that, sir?

THE MAN.   [recovering his charity and self-possession] Bad? Oh no. Human, Master Warder, human. We call one another names when we are offended, as children do. That is all.

THE BEEFEATER.   Ay, sir: words, words, words. Mere wind, sir. We fill our bellies with the east wind, sir, as the Scripture hath it. You cannot feed capons so.

THE MAN.   A good cadence. By your leave [He makes a note of it].

THE BEEFEATER.   What manner of thing is a cadence, sir? I have not heard of it.

THE MAN.   A thing to rule the world with, friend.

THE BEEFEATER.   You speak strangely, sir: no offence. But, an't like you, you are a very civil gentleman; and a poor man feels drawn to you, you being, as twere, willing to share your thought with him.

THE MAN.   Tis my trade. But alas! the world for the most part will none of my thoughts.

Lamplight streams from the palace door as it opens from within.

THE BEEFEATER.   Here comes your lady, sir. I'll to t'other end of my ward. You may een take
your time about your business: I shall
not return too suddenly unless my
sergeant comes prowling round. Tis
a fell sergeant, sir: strict in his arrest.
Go'd'en, sir; and good luck! [He goes].

THE MAN.   "Strict in his arrest"! "Fell sergeant"!
[As if tasting a ripe plum] O-o-o-h!
[He makes a note of them].

A Cloaked Lady gropes her way from
the palace and wanders along the terrace, walking in her sleep.

THE LADY.   [rubbing her hands as if washing
them] Out, damned spot. You will mar
all with these cosmetics. God made
you one face; and you make yourself
another. Think of your grave, woman,
not ever of being beautified. All the
perfumes of Arabia will not whiten
this Tudor hand.

THE MAN.   "All the perfumes of Arabia"! "Beautified"! "Beautified"! a poem in a single
word. Can this be my Mary? [To the
Lady] Why do you speak in a strange
voice, and utter poetry for the first
time? Are you ailing? You walk like the
dead. Mary! Mary!

THE LADY.   [echoing him] Mary! Mary! Who
would have thought that woman to
have had so much blood in her! Is it

my fault that my counsellors put deeds of blood on me? Fie! If you were women you would have more wit than to stain the floor so foully. Hold not up her head so: the hair is false. I tell you yet again, Mary's buried: she cannot come out of her grave. I fear her not: these cats that dare jump into thrones though they be fit only for men's laps must be put away. Whats done cannot be undone. Out, I say. Fie! a queen, and freckled!

THE MAN. [shaking her arm] Mary, I say: art asleep?

The Lady wakes; starts; and nearly faints. He catches her on his arm.

THE LADY. Where am I? What art thou?

THE MAN. I cry your mercy. I have mistook your person all this while. Methought you were my Mary: my mistress.

THE LADY. [outraged] Profane fellow: how do you dare?

THE MAN. Be not wroth with me, lady. My mistress is a marvellous proper woman. But she does not speak so well as you. "All the perfumes of Arabia"! That was well said: spoken with good accent and excellent discretion.

THE LADY. Have I been in speech with you here?

THE MAN. Why, yes, fair lady. Have you forgot it?

THE LADY.   I have walked in my sleep.

THE MAN.   Walk ever in your sleep, fair one; for then your words drop like honey.

THE LADY.   [with cold majesty] Know you to whom you speak, sir, that you dare express yourself so saucily?

THE MAN.   [unabashed] Not I, not care neither. You are some lady of the Court, belike. To me there are but two sorts of women: those with excellent voices, sweet and low, and cackling hens that cannot make me dream. Your voice has all manner of loveliness in it. Grudge me not a short hour of its music.

THE LADY.   Sir: you are overbold. Season your admiration for a while with—

THE MAN.   [holding up his hand to stop her] "Season your admiration for a while—"

THE LADY.   Fellow: do you dare mimic me to my face?

THE MAN.   Tis music. Can you not hear? When a good musician sings a song, do you not sing it and sing it again till you have caught and fixed its perfect melody? "Season your admiration for a while": God! the history of man's heart is in that one word admiration. Admiration! [Taking up his tablets] What was it? "Suspend your admiration for a space—"

THE LADY.   A very vile jingle of esses. I said "Sea-
                   son your—"

THE MAN.   [hastily] Season: ay, season, season,
                   season. Plague on my memory, my
                   wretched memory! I must een write it
                   down. [He begins to write, but stops,
                   his memory failing him]. Yet tell me
                   which was the vile jingle? You said
                   very justly: mine own ear caught it
                   even as my false tongue said it.

THE LADY.   You said "for a space." I said "for a
                   while."

THE MAN.   "For a while" [he corrects it]. Good!
                   [Ardently] And now be mine neither
                   for a space nor a while, but for ever.

THE LADY.   Odds my life! Are you by chance mak-
                   ing love to me, knave?

THE MAN.   Nay: tis you who have made the love:
                   I but pour it out at your feet. I cannot
                   but love a lass that sets such store by
                   an apt word. Therefore vouchsafe, di-
                   vine perfection of a woman—no: I
                   have said that before somewhere; and
                   the wordy garment of my love for you
                   must be fire-new—

THE LADY.   You talk too much, sir. Let me warn
                   you: I am more accustomed to be lis-
                   tened to than preached at.

THE MAN.   The most are like that that do talk well.
                   But though you spake with the tongues
                   of angels, as indeed you do, yet know

that I am the king of words—

THE LADY. A king, ha!

THE MAN. No less. We are poor things, we men and women—

THE LADY. Dare you call me woman?

THE MAN. What nobler name can I tender you? How else can I love you? Yet you may well shrink from the name: have I not said we are but poor things? Yet there is a power that can redeem us.

THE LADY. Gramercy for your sermon, sir. I hope I know my duty.

THE MAN. This is no sermon, but the living truth. The power I speak of is the power of immortal poesy. For know that vile as this world is, and worms as we are, you have but to invest all this vileness with a magical garment of words to transfigure us and uplift our souls til earth flowers into a million heavens.

THE LADY. You spoil your heaven with your million. You are extravagant. Observe some measure in your speech.

THE MAN. You speak now as Ben does.

THE LADY. And who, pray, is Ben?

THE MAN. A learned bricklayer who thinks that the sky is at the top of his ladder, and so takes it on him to rebuke me for flying. I tell you there is no word yet coined and no melody yet sung that is extravagant and majestical enough for the glory that lovely words can reveal. It is heresy to deny it: have you not been taught that in the beginning was the Word? that the Word was with God? nay, that the Word was God?

THE LADY. Beware, fellow, how you presume to speak of holy things. The Queen is the head of the Church.

THE MAN. You are the head of my Church when you speak as you did at first. "All the perfumes of Arabia"! Can the Queen speak thus? They say she playeth well upon the virginals. Let her play so to me; and I'll kiss her hands. But until then, you are my Queen; and I'll kiss those lips that have dropt music on my heart. [He puts his arms about her].

THE LADY. Unmeasured impudence! On your life, take your hands from me.

The Dark Lady comes stooping along the terrace behind them like a running thrush. When she sees how they are employed, she rises angrily to her full height, and listens jealously.

THE MAN. [unaware of the Dark Lady] Then cease to make my hands tremble with the streams of life you pour through them. You hold me as the lodestar holds the iron: I cannot but cling to you. We are lost, you and I: nothing can separate us now.

THE DARK LADY. We shall see that, false lying hound, you and your filthy trull. [With two vigorous cuffs, she knocks the pair asunder, sending the man, who is unlucky enough to receive a righthanded blow, sprawling an the flags]. Take that, both of you!

THE CLOAKED LADY. [in towering wrath, throwing off her cloak and turning in outraged majesty on her assailant] High treason!

THE DARK LADY. [recognizing her and falling on her knees in abject terror] Will: I am lost: I have struck the Queen.

THE MAN. [sitting up as majestically as his ignominious posture allows] Woman: you have struck WILLIAM SHAKE-SPEAR.

QUEEN ELIZABETH. [stupent] Marry, come up!!! Struck William Shakespear quotha! And who in the name of all the sluts and jades and light-o'-loves and fly-by-nights that infest this palace of mine, may William Shakespear be?

THE DARK LADY. Madam: he is but a player. Oh, I could have my hand cut off—

QUEEN ELIZABETH. Belike you will, mistress. Have you bethought you that I am like to have your head cut off as well?

THE DARK LADY.   Will: save me. Oh, save me.

ELIZABETH.   Save you! A likely savior, on my royal word! I had thought this fellow at least an esquire; for I had hoped that even the vilest of my ladies would not have dishonored my Court by wantoning with a baseborn servant.

SHAKESPEAR.   [indignantly scrambling to his feet] Base-born! I, a Shakespear of Stratford! I, whose mother was an Arden! baseborn! You forget yourself, madam.

ELIZABETH.   [furious] S'blood! do I so? I will teach you—

THE DARK LADY.   [rising from her knees and throwing herself between them] Will: in God's name anger her no further. It is death. Madam: do not listen to him.

SHAKESPEAR.   Not were it een to save your life, Mary, not to mention mine own, will I flatter a monarch who forgets what is due to my family. I deny not that my father was brought down to be a poor bankrupt; but twas his gentle blood that was ever too generous for trade. Never did he disown his debts. Tis true he paid them not; but it is an attested truth that he gave bills for them; and twas those bills, in the hands of base hucksters, that were his undoing.

ELIZABETH.   [grimly] The son of your father shall learn his place in the presence of the daughter of Harry the Eighth.

| SHAKESPEAR. | [swelling with intolerant importance] Name not that inordinate man in the same breath with Stratford's worthiest alderman. John Shakespear wedded but once: Harry Tudor was married six times. You should blush to utter his name. |

SHAKESPEAR.   [swelling with intolerant importance] Name not that inordinate man in the same breath with Stratford's worthiest alderman. John Shakespear wedded but once: Harry Tudor was married six times. You should blush to utter his name.

THE DARK LADY.   Will: for pity's sake— crying out together

ELIZABETH.   Insolent dog—

SHAKESPEAR.   [cutting them short] How know you that King Harry was indeed your father?

ELIZABETH.   Zounds! Now by—she stops to grind her teeth with rage].

THE DARK LADY.   She will have me whipped through the streets. Oh God! Oh God!

SHAKESPEAR.   Learn to know yourself better, madam. I am an honest gentleman of unquestioned parentage, and have already sent in my demand for the coat-of-arms that is lawfully mine. Can you say as much for yourself?

ELIZABETH.   [almost beside herself] Another word; and I begin with mine own hands the work the hangman shall finish.

SHAKESPEAR.   You are no true Tudor: this baggage here has as good a right to your royal seat as you. What maintains you on the throne of England? Is it your renowned wit? your wisdom that sets at naught the craftiest statesmen of the Christian world? No. Tis the mere chance that might have happened to any milkmaid, the caprice of Nature that made you the most wondrous piece of beauty the age hath seen. [Elizabeth's raised fists, on the point of striking him, fall to her side]. That is what hath brought all men to your feet, and founded your throne on the impregnable rock of your proud heart, a stony island in a sea of desire. There, madam, is some wholesome blunt honest speaking for you. Now do your worst.

ELIZABETH. [with dignity] Master Shakespear: it is well for you that I am a merciful prince. I make allowance for your rustic ignorance. But remember that there are things which be true, and are yet not seemly to be said (I will not say to a queen; for you will have it that I am none) but to a virgin.

SHAKESPEAR. [bluntly] It is no fault of mine that you are a virgin, madam, albeit tis my misfortune.

THE DARK LADY. [terrified again] In mercy, madam, hold no further discourse with him. He hath ever some lewd jest on his tongue. You hear how he useth me! calling me baggage and the like to your

Majesty's face.

ELIZABETH. As for you, mistress, I have yet to demand what your business is at this hour in this place, and how you come to be so concerned with a player that you strike blindly at your sovereign in your jealousy of him.

THE DARK LADY. Madam: as I live and hope for salvation—

SHAKESPEAR. [sardonically] Ha!

THE DARK LADY. [angrily]—ay, I'm as like to be saved as thou that believest naught save some black magic of words and verses—I say, madam, as I am a living woman I came here to break with him for ever. Oh, madam, if you would know what misery is, listen to this man that is more than man and less at the same time. He will tie you down to anatomize your very soul: he will wring tears of blood from your humiliation; and then he will heal the wound with flatteries that no woman can resist.

SHAKESPEAR. Flatteries! [Kneeling] Oh, madam, I put my case at your royal feet. I confess to much. I have a rude tongue: I am unmannerly: I blaspheme against the holiness of anointed royalty; but oh, my royal mistress, AM I a flatterer?

ELIZABETH. I absolve you as to that. You are far too plain a dealer to please me. [He rises gratefully].

THE DARK LADY.

Madam: he is flattering you even as he speaks.

ELIZABETH.

[a terrible flash in her eye] Ha! Is it so?

SHAKESPEAR.

Madam: she is jealous; and, heaven help me! not without reason. Oh, you say you are a merciful prince; but that was cruel of you, that hiding of your royal dignity when you found me here. For how can I ever be content with this black-haired, black-eyed, black-avised devil again now that I have looked upon real beauty and real majesty?

THE DARK LADY.

[wounded and desperate] He hath swore to me ten times over that the day shall come in England when black women, for all their foulness, shall be more thought on than fair ones. [To Shakespear, scolding at him] Deny it if thou canst. Oh, he is compact of lies and scorns. I am tired of being tossed up to heaven and dragged down to hell at every whim that takes him. I am ashamed to my very soul that I have abased myself to love one that my father would not have deemed fit to hold my stirrup—one that will talk to all the world about me—that will put my love and my shame into his plays and make me blush for myself there—that will write sonnets about me that no man of gentle strain would put his hand to. I am all disordered: I know not what I am saying to your Majesty: I am of all ladies most deject and wretched—

SHAKESPEAR. Ha! At last sorrow hath struck a note of music out of thee. "Of all ladies most deject and wretched." [He makes a note of it].

THE DARK LADY. Madam: I implore you give me leave to go. I am distracted with grief and shame. I—

ELIZABETH. Go [The Dark Lady tries to kiss her hand]. No more. Go. [The Dark Lady goes, convulsed]. You have been cruel to that poor fond wretch, Master SHAKESPEAR.

SHAKESPEAR. I am not cruel, madam; but you know the fable of Jupiter and Semele. I could not help my lightnings scorching her.

ELIZABETH. You have an overweening conceit of yourself, sir, that displeases your Queen.

SHAKESPEAR. Oh, madam, can I go about with the modest cough of a minor poet, belittling my inspiration and making the mightiest wonder of your reign a thing of nought? I have said that "not marble nor the gilded monuments of princes shall outlive" the words with which I make the world glorious or foolish at my will. Besides, I would have you think me great enough to grant me a boon.

ELIZABETH. I hope it is a boon that may be asked of a virgin Queen without offence, sir. I mistrust your forwardness; and I bid you remember that I do not suffer persons of your degree (if I may say so without offence to your father the alderman) to presume too far.

SHAKESPEAR. Oh, madam, I shall not forget myself again; though by my life, could I make you a serving wench, neither a queen nor a virgin should you be for so much longer as a flash of lightning might take to cross the river to the Bankside. But since you are a queen and will none of me, nor of Philip of Spain, nor of any other mortal man, I must een contain myself as best I may, and ask you only for a boon of State.

ELIZABETH. A boon of State already! You are becoming a courtier like the rest of them. You lack advancement.

SHAKESPEAR. "Lack advancement." By your Majesty's leave: a queenly phrase. [He is about to write it down].

ELIZABETH. [striking the tablets from his hand] Your tables begin to anger me, sir. I am not here to write your plays for you.

SHAKESPEAR. You are here to inspire them, madam. For this, among the rest, were you ordained. But the boon I crave is that

<table>
<tr><td></td><td>you do endow a great playhouse, or, if I may make bold to coin a scholarly name for it, a National Theatre, for the better instruction and gracing of your Majesty's subjects.</td></tr>
<tr><td>ELIZABETH.</td><td>Why, sir, are there not theatres enow on the Bankside and in Blackfriars?</td></tr>
<tr><td>SHAKESPEAR.</td><td>Madam: these are the adventures of needy and desperate men that must, to save themselves from perishing of want, give the sillier sort of people what they best like; and what they best like, God knows, is not their own betterment and instruction, as we well see by the example of the churches, which must needs compel men to frequent them, though they be open to all without charge. Only when there is a matter of a murder, or a plot, or a pretty youth in petticoats, or some naughty tale of wantonness, will your subjects pay the great cost of good players and their finery, with a little profit to boot. To prove this I will tell you that I have written two noble and excellent plays setting forth the advancement of women of high nature and fruitful industry even as your Majesty is: the one a skilful physician, the other a sister devoted to good works. I have also stole from a book of idle wanton tales two of the most damnable foolishnesses in the world, in the one of which</td></tr>
</table>

a woman goeth in man's attire and maketh impudent love to her swain, who pleaseth the groundlings by overthrowing a wrestler; whilst, in the other, one of the same kidney sheweth her wit by saying endless naughtinesses to a gentleman as lewd as herself. I have writ these to save my friends from penury, yet shewing my scorn for such follies and for them that praise them by calling the one As You Like It, meaning that it is not as I like it, and the other Much Ado About Nothing, as it truly is. And now these two filthy pieces drive their nobler fellows from the stage, where indeed I cannot have my lady physician presented at all, she being too honest a woman for the taste of the town. Wherefore I humbly beg your Majesty to give order that a theatre be endowed out of the public revenue for the playing of those pieces of mine which no merchant will touch, seeing that his gain is so much greater with the worse than with the better. Thereby you shall also encourage other men to undertake the writing of plays who do now despise it and leave it wholly to those whose counsels will work little good to your realm. For this writing of plays is a great matter, forming as it does the minds and affections of men in such sort that whatsoever they see done in show on the stage, they will presently be doing in earnest in the world, which is but a larger stage. Of late, as you know, the Church taught the people by means of plays; but the people flocked only to such as were full of superstitious miracles and bloody martyrdoms; and so the Church, which also was just then brought into straits by the policy of your royal father, did abandon and discountenance the art of playing; and thus it fell into the hands of poor players and greedy merchants that had their pockets to look to and not the greatness of this your kingdom. Therefore now must your Majesty take up that good work that your Church hath abandoned, and restore the art of playing to its former use and dignity.

ELIZABETH. Master Shakespear: I will speak of this matter to the Lord Treasurer.

SHAKESPEAR. Then am I undone, madam; for there was never yet a Lord Treasurer that could find a penny for anything over and above the necessary expenses of your government, save for a war or a salary for his own nephew.

ELIZABETH. Master Shakespear: you speak sooth; yet cannot I in any wise mend it. I dare not offend my unruly Puritans by making so lewd a place as the playhouse a public charge; and there be a thousand things to be done in this London of mine before your poetry can have its penny from the general purse. I tell thee, Master Will, it will be three hundred years and more before my subjects learn that man cannot live by bread alone, but by every word that cometh from the mouth of those whom God inspires. By that time you and I will be dust beneath the feet of the horses, if indeed there be any horses then, and men be still riding instead of flying. Now it may be that by then your works will be dust also.

SHAKESPEAR. They will stand, madam: fear nor for that.

ELIZABETH. It may prove so. But of this I am certain (for I know my countrymen) that until every other country in the Christian world, even to barbarian Muscovy and the hamlets of the boorish Germans, have its playhouse at the public charge, England will never adventure. And she will adventure then only because it is her desire to be ever in the fashion, and to do humbly and dutifully whatso she seeth everybody else doing. In the meantime you must content yourself as best you can by the playing of those two pieces which you give out as the most damnable ever writ, but which your countrymen, I warn you, will swear are the best you have ever done. But this I will say, that if I could speak across the ages to our descendants, I should heartily recommend them to fulfil your wish; for the Scottish minstrel hath well said that he that maketh the songs of a nation is mightier than he that maketh its laws; and the same may well be true of plays and interludes. [The clock chimes the first quarter. The warder returns on his round]. And now, sir, we are upon the hour when it better beseems a virgin queen to be abed than to converse alone with the naughtiest of her subjects. Ho there! Who keeps ward on the queen's lodgings tonight?

THE WARDER. I do, an't please your majesty.

ELIZABETH. See that you keep it better in future. You have let pass a most dangerous gallant even to the very door of our royal chamber. Lead him forth; and bring me word when he is safely locked out; for I shall scarce dare disrobe until the palace gates are between us.

SHAKESPEAR. [kissing her hand] My body goes through the gate into the darkness, madam; but my thoughts follow you.

ELIZABETH. How! to my bed!

SHAKESPEAR. No, madam, to your prayers, in which I beg you to remember my theatre.

ELIZABETH.   That is my prayer to posterity. Forget
                    not your own to God; and so good-
                    night, Master Will.

SHAKESPEAR.   Goodnight, great ELIZABETH.
                    God save the Queen!

ELIZABETH.   Amen.

Exeunt severally: she to her chamber: he, in custody of the
warer, to the gate nearest Blackfriars.

AYOT, ST. LAWRENCE, 20th June 1910.